This book
belongs to

_____

Barbie™
Story Treasury

EGMONT

We bring stories to life

Barbie in The Nutcracker first published in the United States in 2001 by Pleasant Company Publications.

Barbie as The Princess and the Pauper first published in the United States in 2004 by Golden Books,
an imprint of Random House Children's Books.

Barbie as Rapunzel first published in the United States in 2002 by Pleasant Company Publications.

Barbie in Swan Lake first published in the United States in 2003 by Golden Books,
an imprint of Random House Children's Books.

Barbie Story Treasury first published in Great Britain in 2006 by Dean, an imprint of Egmont UK Limited,
239 Kensington High Street, London W8 6SA.
BARBIE and associated trademarks and trade dress are owned by and used under licence from Mattel, Inc.
© 2006 Mattel, Inc

1 3 5 7 9 10 8 6 4 2
ISBN 0 6035 6244 2
ISBN 978 0 6035 6244 0

Printed in Singapore

Barbie™
Story Treasury

DEAN

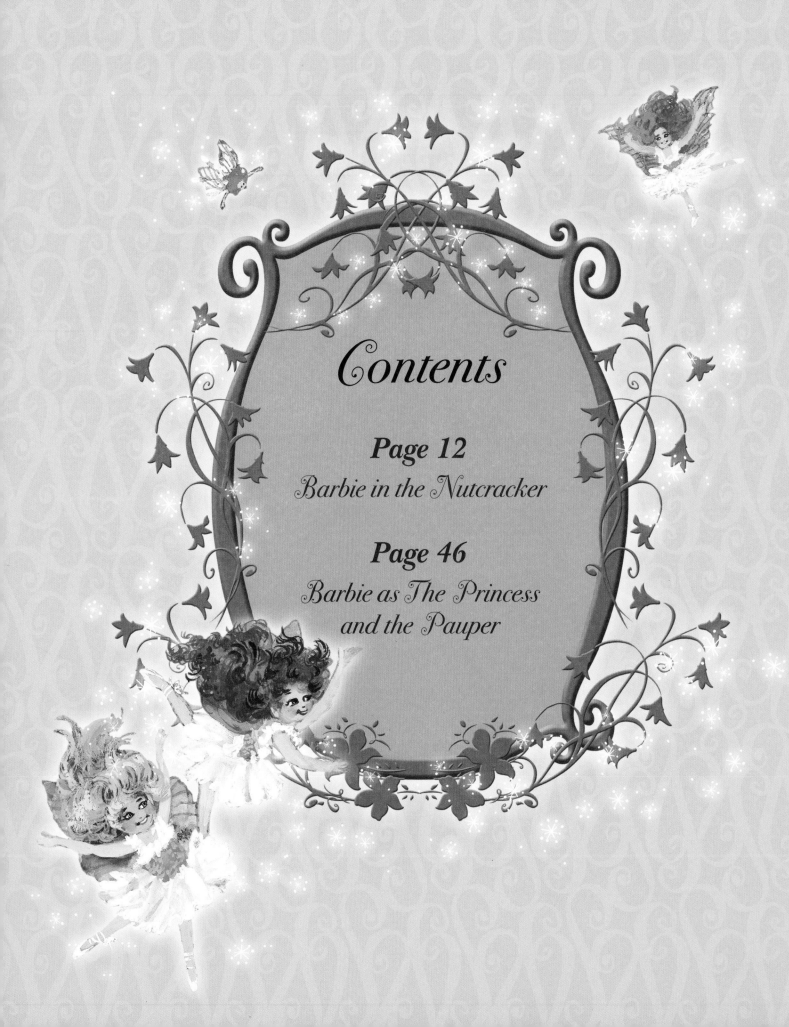

Contents

Barbie™ in the Nutcracker

Barbie stars as Clara, a beautiful girl who receives a magical Nutcracker as a Christmas present. That night, she wakes up to find that the Nutcracker has come to life, and is fighting with an army of mice. Clara tries to help, but the evil Mouse King casts a spell to shrink her to the Nutcracker's size.

Clara and the enchanted Nutcracker set out on a series of magical adventures, searching for the Sugarplum Princess, who can free them from the evil spell.

Barbie™
IN THE
Nutcracker

FROM THE ORIGINAL VIDEO SCREENPLAY BY

LINDA ENGELSIEPEN & HILARY HINKLE

BASED ON THE CLASSIC TALE BY

E. T. A. HOFFMAN

ILLUSTRATED BY

ROBERT SAUBER

One Christmas Eve, a long time ago, a girl named Clara received a special present from her favourite aunt: a fine wooden Nutcracker. "Thank you, Auntie!" Clara cried. "He's wonderful!" But just a short time later, Clara's jealous little brother Tommy yanked the Nutcracker's arm, causing it to snap!

That night, Clara tiptoed downstairs and carefully bandaged the Nutcracker's arm. She soon drifted to sleep on the soft parlour sofa. As she dreamed, the clock began to strike midnight. *Bong! Bong! Bong!* Sparkling mist poured from a tiny knothole in the clock. *Bong! Bong! Bong!* An army of mice swarmed into the room.

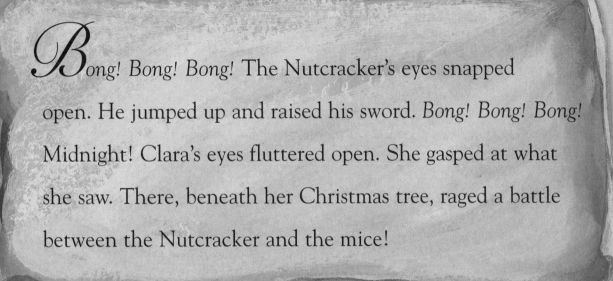

*B*ong! *Bong! Bong!* The Nutcracker's eyes snapped open. He jumped up and raised his sword. *Bong! Bong! Bong!* Midnight! Clara's eyes fluttered open. She gasped at what she saw. There, beneath her Christmas tree, raged a battle between the Nutcracker and the mice!

Clara tried to help. But the Mouse King cast a spell, and Clara began to shrink until she was as small as the Nutcracker. "Only the Sugarplum Princess can undo this spell," the Nutcracker told her. "I've been searching for the princess ever since the Mouse King turned me into a Nutcracker."

Just then, an owl gave Clara a shiny locket. "When you find the Sugarplum Princess," he explained, "open the locket, and you will return home your normal size."

*T*ogether, Clara and the Nutcracker went in search of the Sugarplum Princess – through the knothole in the clock, then down a sparkling tunnel that led to a magical land. Snowflakes glittered, but it wasn't even cold! Suddenly, they were surrounded by tiny, dancing creatures. "Snow fairies," the Nutcracker said.

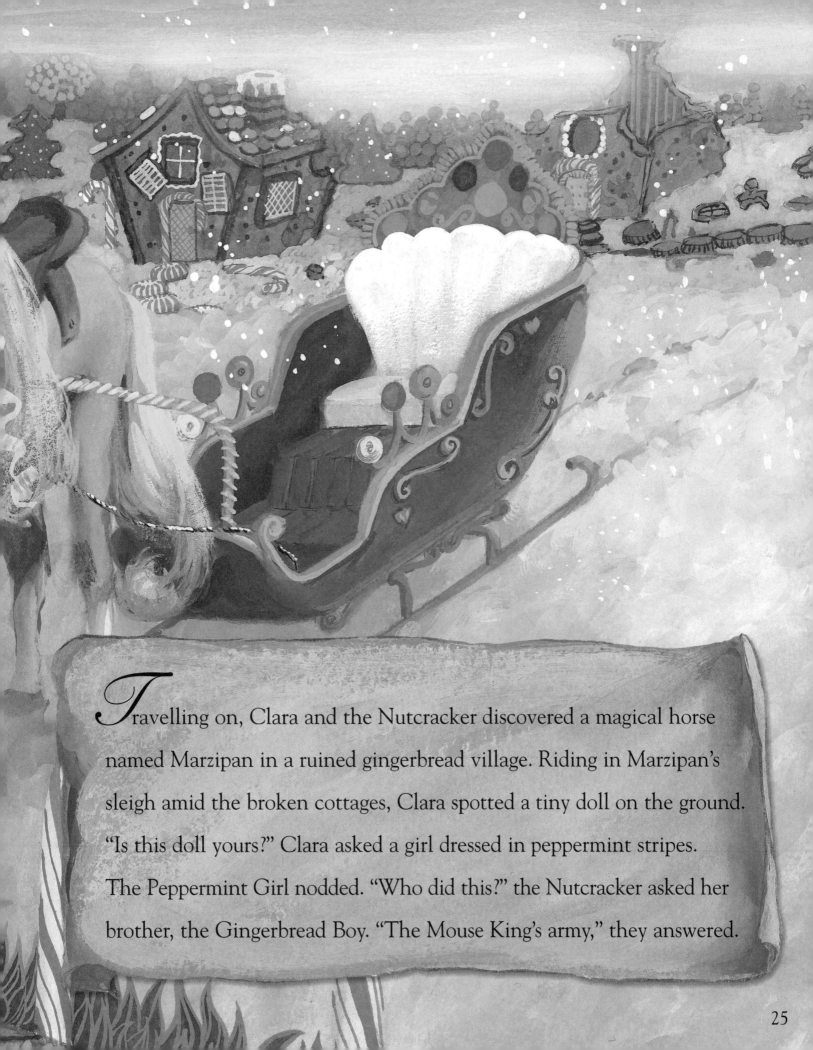

Travelling on, Clara and the Nutcracker discovered a magical horse named Marzipan in a ruined gingerbread village. Riding in Marzipan's sleigh amid the broken cottages, Clara spotted a tiny doll on the ground. "Is this doll yours?" Clara asked a girl dressed in peppermint stripes. The Peppermint Girl nodded. "Who did this?" the Nutcracker asked her brother, the Gingerbread Boy. "The Mouse King's army," they answered.

"And here they come!" yelled the children. Marzipan raced away for safety, leaving Clara and her friends to run from the evil mice. Suddenly, a ladder unfurled from a tree above. Racing up the ladder, they met their rescuers, Major Mint and Colonel Candy. "Let us help you find the Sugarplum Princess," said Major Mint.

Meanwhile, inside the Palace of Sweets, the Mouse King sat surrounded by subjects he'd turned into stone. Frowning, he listened as Pimm the Bat told him the news: Clara and the Nutcracker were looking for the Sugarplum Princess. The Mouse King's eyes glittered. "I have a plan to stop them!" he sneered.

$\mathcal{B}$ack in the forest, Clara and the Nutcracker searched for food and water for their journey. When the Nutcracker uncovered an old well, dozens of flower fairies escaped. The fairies, who'd been trapped by the evil mice, danced to thank the Nutcracker for setting them free. Filled with delight, Clara joined the fairies' fun.

Suddenly, the ground began to shake. The Mouse King had sent a Rock Giant to attack!

The air filled with snow. No, not snow – the snow fairies! They blew on the nearby lake, turning it to ice. And Marzipan galloped back, too. "Hurry to the sleigh!" Clara cried. As the Nutcracker cracked the ice with his sword, the Rock Giant crashed into the dark, icy water.

The group travelled on into a thick, dark fog. Soon, through the mist, they spotted an island of silver and gold – and a palace that glistened like pearls! "The Sugarplum Palace!" Major Mint cried, and he led them into the castle. But suddenly the castle melted away. Clara saw that it was a trick! Her friends were trapped in a huge cage! She watched in horror as grey bats unfolded their wings and carried her friends away.

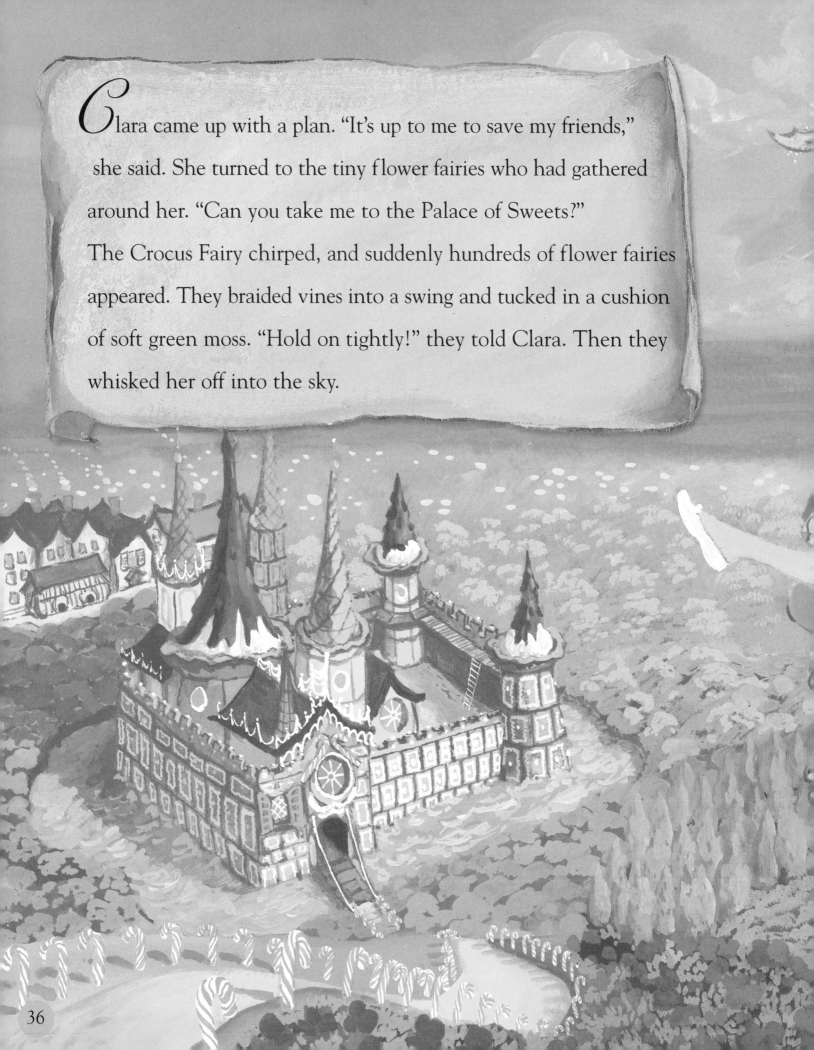

Clara came up with a plan. "It's up to me to save my friends," she said. She turned to the tiny flower fairies who had gathered around her. "Can you take me to the Palace of Sweets?"

The Crocus Fairy chirped, and suddenly hundreds of flower fairies appeared. They braided vines into a swing and tucked in a cushion of soft green moss. "Hold on tightly!" they told Clara. Then they whisked her off into the sky.

When Clara reached the castle, she sneaked inside
and saved her friends. The Mouse King was angered by their
escape. He called to his soldiers and aimed his magic sceptre.
But the Nutcracker raised his sword and the blade reflected
the evil magic back at the Mouse King – and he began to
shrink and shrink and shrink . . .

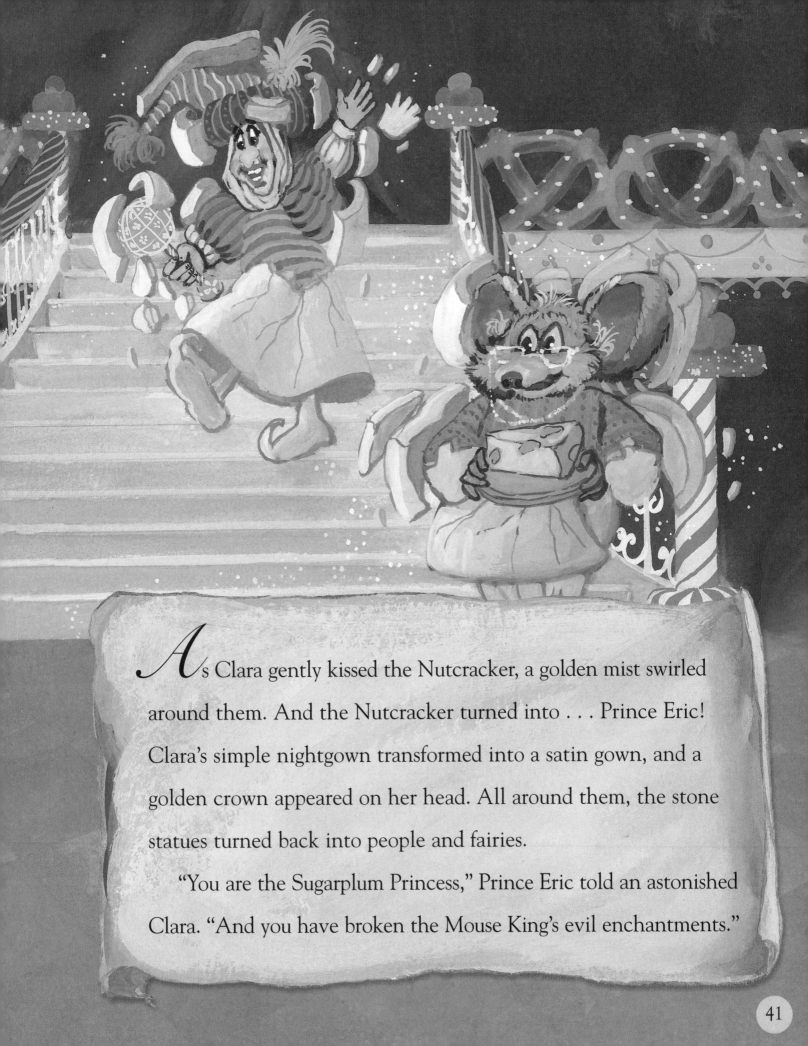

As Clara gently kissed the Nutcracker, a golden mist swirled around them. And the Nutcracker turned into . . . Prince Eric! Clara's simple nightgown transformed into a satin gown, and a golden crown appeared on her head. All around them, the stone statues turned back into people and fairies.

"You are the Sugarplum Princess," Prince Eric told an astonished Clara. "And you have broken the Mouse King's evil enchantments."

The fairies transformed the palace with magic. Everyone celebrated, then bowed as the prince was crowned king.

"Will you stay and be my queen?" King Eric asked Clara. Clara grasped the locket around her neck. "This was supposed to take me home. But in my heart, I feel I'm already there." The teeny tiny Mouse King was not finished with his mischief, however. Pimm the Bat swooped down and stole Clara's locket and handed it to the Mouse King. And as he opened it, Clara began to fade away . . .

43

When Clara awoke, it was Christmas morning. She was back home, in the parlour, without her locket, and the Nutcracker had disappeared. She was so sad, she didn't even care that she had to wait for her favourite aunt to arrive before they could open presents.

Later that evening, her aunt finally arrived – but with a friend. "I'd like you to meet . . . Eric," she said with a smile.

Clara gasped. "It's you, isn't it?" she whispered. Eric smiled and slipped something into the palm of her hand. Her missing locket! "May I have the next dance?" he asked. And as they danced, Clara felt as if they were the king and queen of their very own fairy-tale castle.

45

Barbie™ as the Princess and the Pauper

Princess Anneliese goes walking one day, and is amazed to come across a girl who looks just like she does - the poor seamstress, Erika. Meanwhile, the royal advisor, Preminger, is plotting to become king.

Preminger kidnaps Anneliese, and tells the Queen she has run away. But Erika impersonates the Princess, and with the help of Anneliese's tutor, Julian, the two girls foil Preminger's evil plot.

Barbie™ as The Princess and the Pauper

BY
Mary Man Kong

FROM THE ORIGINAL SCREENPLAY BY
CLIFF RUBY & ELANA LESSER

ILLUSTRATED BY
Lisa Falkenstern

Special thanks to Rob Hudnut, Shelley Tabbut, Vicki Jaeger,
Monica Lopez, Jesyca C. Durchin, and Mainframe Entertainment.

ong ago and far away, two lovely little girls were born. Erika grew up in a small village, toiling as a seamstress. Anneliese grew up in a big, beautiful palace, learning her royal duties as a princess. They led very different lives, but they looked exactly the same – except for their hair colour.

One day, the Queen discovered that the royal gold mines were empty. She wanted her daughter, Anneliese, to marry the rich King Dominick so that there would be enough money to take care of all the people in the kingdom. Princess Anneliese, however, was in love with her tutor, Julian.

"I wish I were free to do what I want," Princess Anneliese said as she and Julian walked through the village.

Suddenly, they heard beautiful singing – it was Erika. The Princess saw Erika and thought she was looking in a mirror!

"You look just like me," Princess Anneliese told Erika. "Except for our hair colour and this crown-shaped birthmark on my shoulder, we could be twins."

The two girls quickly became friends. The Princess learned that Erika had to pay off her parents' debt and worked at Madame Carp's dress shop. Before saying goodbye, Anneliese promised to have Erika sing at the palace one day.

51

Meanwhile, no one knew that the royal advisor, Preminger, had stolen the Queen's gold. He was now rich, and he wanted the Princess to marry him to save the kingdom. More than anything, he wanted to be king.

When Preminger learned that the Princess was going to marry King Dominick, he was furious! He had the Princess kidnapped and taken to an abandoned royal cabin. He then told the Queen that Princess Anneliese had run away. Preminger hoped that King Dominick would call off the wedding. And the Queen would be so grateful when Preminger later returned the Princess that she would let him marry her daughter.

Julian didn't believe Preminger's story. He went to Madame Carp's dress shop and asked Erika to help him.

"Me? What can I do?" Erika asked.

"Pretend to be Princess Anneliese while I find out what's going on," said Julian.

"Who would ever believe I'm a princess?" asked Erika.

"Leave that to me," Julian said, smiling.

So with a blond wig and some coaching, Erika learned how to walk, act, and dress like the Princess.

Julian went back to the palace and announced that the Princess had returned. When King Dominick was introduced to Erika, he fell in love with her beautiful voice and sweet nature. Erika fell in love with the King because he was gentle and kind.

"There's something about you," King Dominick said. "You're honest and down-to-earth. You don't act like a princess."

Erika wished she could tell the King the truth, but first Julian had to find the real Princess.

At the royal cabin, Princess Anneliese planned her escape.
Covering her cat, Serafina, with a white sheet, the Princess called
to her kidnappers, "Help! A ghost!"

When Preminger's men rushed to open the door, Serafina
dropped the sheet over them. The Princess and Serafina then fled
to the palace.

Everyone at the palace believed that Erika was the Princess – even Preminger. He raced to the cabin to see what had happened to Princess Anneliese. Julian secretly followed him.

Preminger was furious when he discovered that Anneliese was gone.

"Where is the Princess, Preminger?" Julian demanded. "What have you done with her?"

"You're the tutor. You should have all the answers," Preminger replied as his men captured Julian.

Princess Anneliese made her way back to the palace gates. But seeing her stained and dirty clothes, no one believed she was the Princess. The guards wouldn't let her in! With nowhere else to turn, Anneliese went to Madame Carp's dress shop to see if Erika could help her.

Madame Carp saw the Princess and thought she was Erika. "You lazy girl!" the old dressmaker scolded. "You're not leaving until every dress is finished."

Then Madame Carp locked Princess Anneliese in the shop.

The Princess tried to send a message to the palace. She tied her royal ring to one of Madame Carp's dress labels and attached it to Serafina's collar.

"Take this to the palace," Princess Anneliese instructed her cat. "When they see the label, it will lead them here."

Unfortunately, Preminger found Serafina first. He went to Madame Carp's shop and pretended that he wanted to help Princess Anneliese. But instead of returning her to the palace, he took the Princess to the abandoned gold mine.

When Princess Anneliese found Julian tied up, she realized that Preminger was behind her own kidnapping.

"Now I'm going to tell the Queen you've been in an unfortunate mining accident and she'll have to marry me to save the kingdom," Preminger said.

"No one will believe you," said Princess Anneliese.

"They will when they see this!" Preminger laughed as he showed them the Princess's ring.

Preminger left the mine and had his men knock down the beams leading to the entrance. Princess Anneliese and Julian were trapped!

At the palace, King Dominick offered Erika a beautiful engagement ring and asked her to marry him.

"But that girl isn't the Princess," Preminger announced. "She's an impostor!"

"What proof do you have?" asked King Dominick.

Suddenly, Preminger's dog, Midas, jumped up and pulled off Erika's wig.

"And look at her shoulder," Preminger directed. "There's no royal birthmark. Take her to the dungeon!"

The King's ambassador was outraged. He made the King leave the palace immediately.

Preminger held up Princess Anneliese's royal ring. He told the Queen the Princess was dead.

"What will I do without my daughter?" cried the Queen. "What will become of my kingdom now?"

"I can save your kingdom," said Preminger. "I've made quite a bit of money in my businesses. Marry me and your problem will be solved."

Reluctantly, the Queen agreed.

Meanwhile, the Princess and Julian were desperately trying to find a way out of the gold mine. Suddenly, Erika's cat, Wolfie, appeared. The clever cat led them toward an old mine shaft, but they couldn't climb to the opening – it was too steep.

As they stopped to rest, Anneliese noticed a rock that had split open, showing sparkling crystals.

"Look! Geodes!" exclaimed the Princess. "I never knew we had them in the mine."

Julian swung his pickaxe and dislodged some of the rocks near a bubbling pool of water. The water shot up like a geyser.

"That's the way out!" shouted Anneliese. The water filled the mine and lifted them through the shaft to freedom.

Meanwhile, Erika sang a beautiful song that slowly put the guards in the dungeon to sleep. She then tiptoed out, right into the arms of – King Dominick! He was dressed as a guard and had returned to rescue her.

"What are you doing here?" Erika asked the King.

"I don't care if you're not the Princess," King Dominick said. "I like you for being who you are."

"You're the first person who's ever believed in me," said Erika. As she spoke, she realized that the King was in love with her.

But there was no time to waste – the palace guards would soon realize that Erika was missing. The King and Erika ran to his horse and rode off to safety.

The wedding of Preminger and the Queen was about to begin when Princess Anneliese burst in.

"Stop the wedding!" Anneliese shouted.

"It's the impostor!" Preminger exclaimed.

"No, Preminger," the Princess said as she showed everyone the crown-shaped birthmark on her shoulder. "I'm Princess Anneliese, and I'm alive!"

Knowing that his evil plan was falling apart, Preminger tried to escape. He jumped onto his horse, Herve, and raced away. But Herve realized that Preminger was evil and galloped right back to the palace. When the horse finally stopped short, Preminger landed in the royal wedding cake and was quickly arrested.

"When I think what might have happened . . ." The Queen shuddered.

"But it didn't, thanks to Erika and Julian," Princess Anneliese said. "Julian is the man I love. He had Erika pretend to be me so he could save me."

"I want you to be happy," the Queen told her. "But the kingdom is in trouble."

"Don't worry, Mother. The gold mine isn't worthless after all," the Princess explained. "We found geodes in the mines. They're very valuable and will save the kingdom!"

Then the Princess thanked Erika and paid off the girl's debt at Madame Carp's shop. Erika was free!

King Dominick proposed to Erika. And after following her dream of singing and travelling the world, she returned to marry the King. That spring, the most beautiful double wedding the kingdom had ever seen took place. Princess Anneliese married Julian, and Erika married King Dominick. Serafina and Wolfie had many, many kittens together. And they all lived happily ever after.

Barbie™ as Rapunzel

Rapunzel is a servant girl with beautiful, shining long hair.
She keeps house for the evil witch, Gothel, helped by her friends Penelope,
the little dragon, and Hobie, the rabbit. Gothel has never told her about the
world outside, but one day Rapunzel discovers a secret passage and meets with
a handsome prince.

The witch tries everything she can to keep her imprisoned, but Rapunzel never
gives up on her dream of escaping the tower and finding Prince Stefan again.

Barbie™

— AS —

Rapunzel

FROM THE ORIGINAL SCREENPLAY BY

Cliff Ruby & Elana Lesser

BASED ON THE CLASSIC TALE BY

The Brothers Grimm

ILLUSTRATED BY

Robert Sauber

Once there was a girl named Rapunzel who had beautiful long hair and loved to paint. She was a servant of a jealous, scheming witch named Gothel, who made her work hard every day. "I took you in when nobody else wanted you or loved you," Gothel always reminded her. The witch kept Rapunzel hidden away in a grand manor guarded by an enormous dragon named Hugo.

Rapunzel's best friends – Penelope, Hugo's daughter, and Hobie, a gruff but good-hearted rabbit – were always by her side and tried to help her. But no matter how hard Rapunzel worked, Gothel was never pleased.

One day Rapunzel and her friends discovered a secret stairwell beneath the kitchen floor. Curious, they crept down the stairs and found an old wooden chest. Inside the chest was a beautiful silver hairbrush with a poem engraved on the handle:

> Constant as the stars above,
> Always know that you are loved.
> To our daughter, Rapunzel, on her first birthday,
> With love forever, Mother and Father.

Rapunzel nearly wept. "Gothel said my parents never loved me . . . that I was left on her doorstep when I was a tiny baby. Why would she have lied to me?"

Suddenly Penelope sneezed and left a smoking hole in the floor – revealing a secret tunnel! Rapunzel crawled through the dark passage till it opened into the forest. Just beyond the forest stood a charming village. And in the distance, a gleaming white castle rose against the sky! Rapunzel was amazed. It was all so beautiful – and so close-by. Why had Gothel told her there was no one living around them for miles?

As Rapunzel walked toward the castle gardens, she saw a young girl start to fall into a pit. Quickly, she ran to the girl and pulled her to safety, but then Rapunzel began to slip into the pit, too! Suddenly, strong arms caught her. She had been rescued by the girl's brother. Rapunzel longed to stay and talk to him, but she feared Gothel would discover her missing. So she ran back into the tunnel without finding out the young man's name. What she did not know was that the girl was a princess and that her brother was a prince – Prince Stefan.

Back at the manor, Gothel's spying ferret, Otto, had already told tales on Rapunzel, and the witch was waiting for her when she returned. "How dare you!" Gothel fumed.

"What are you hiding?" Rapunzel asked her. "You can't keep me locked away from the world forever."

"Watch me!" grinned Gothel. With a magical bolt from her fingertips, she made the door disappear, the stairs vanish, and the wall grow. Gothel then destroyed Rapunzel's easel and paints. The long-haired beauty found herself trapped in a tall tower.

Gothel called Hugo to her. "See to it that she stays put . . . or else," the witch warned him.

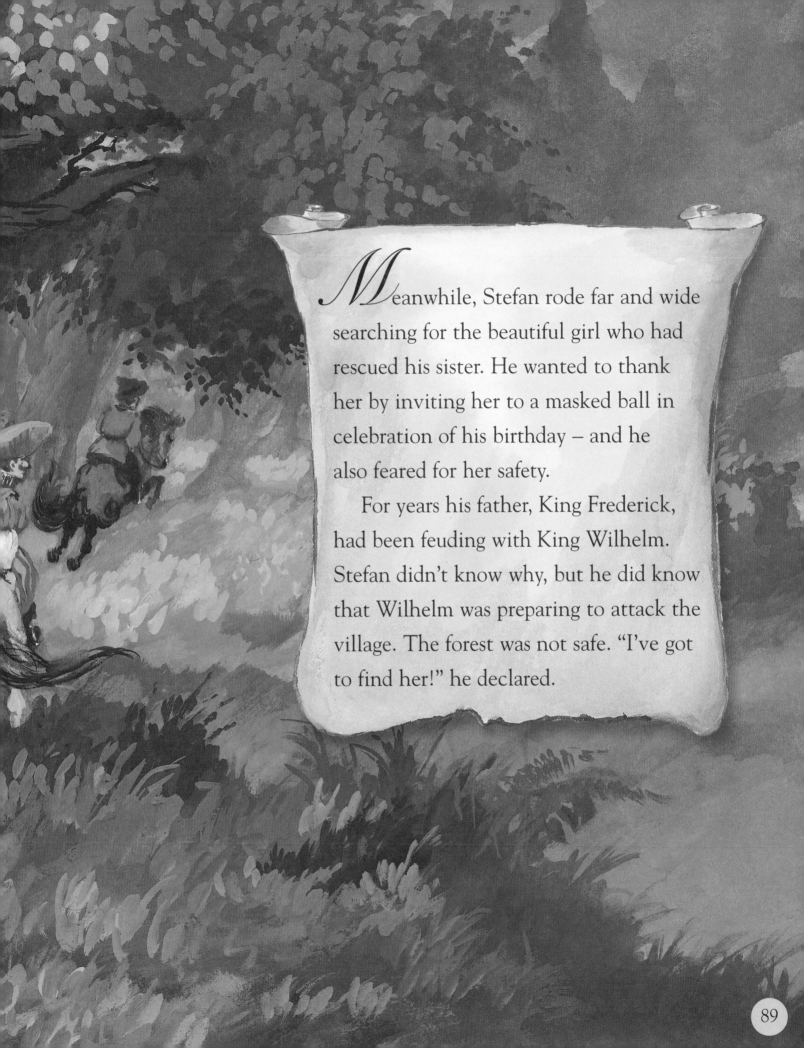

Meanwhile, Stefan rode far and wide searching for the beautiful girl who had rescued his sister. He wanted to thank her by inviting her to a masked ball in celebration of his birthday – and he also feared for her safety.

For years his father, King Frederick, had been feuding with King Wilhelm. Stefan didn't know why, but he did know that Wilhelm was preparing to attack the village. The forest was not safe. "I've got to find her!" he declared.

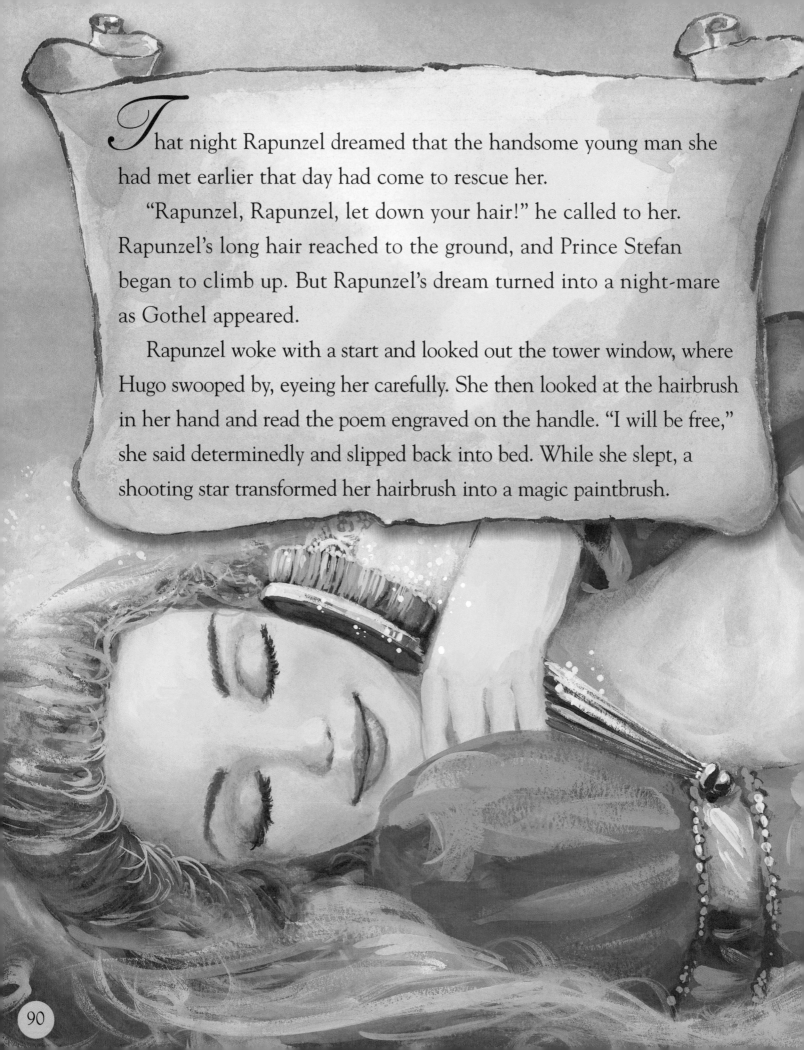

That night Rapunzel dreamed that the handsome young man she had met earlier that day had come to rescue her.

"Rapunzel, Rapunzel, let down your hair!" he called to her. Rapunzel's long hair reached to the ground, and Prince Stefan began to climb up. But Rapunzel's dream turned into a night-mare as Gothel appeared.

Rapunzel woke with a start and looked out the tower window, where Hugo swooped by, eyeing her carefully. She then looked at the hairbrush in her hand and read the poem engraved on the handle. "I will be free," she said determinedly and slipped back into bed. While she slept, a shooting star transformed her hairbrush into a magic paintbrush.

The next morning, Penelope and Hobie brought Rapunzel new paints to cheer her up. It was then that Rapunzel discovered her hairbrush had changed into a paintbrush. Curious, she dipped the brush into the paint and began painting a mural of the garden where she had met Prince Stefan. When she was finished, Rapunzel and her friends were astonished. The painting looked real!

Rapunzel touched the painting – and her hand passed right through! "Maybe you shouldn't do that," Penelope and Hobie cautioned. But in her heart, Rapunzel knew that it was safe. She stepped through the painting, right into the garden – and into Prince Stefan's path.

"I've been looking everywhere for you!" he exclaimed. He handed her a scroll with an invitation to the masked ball.

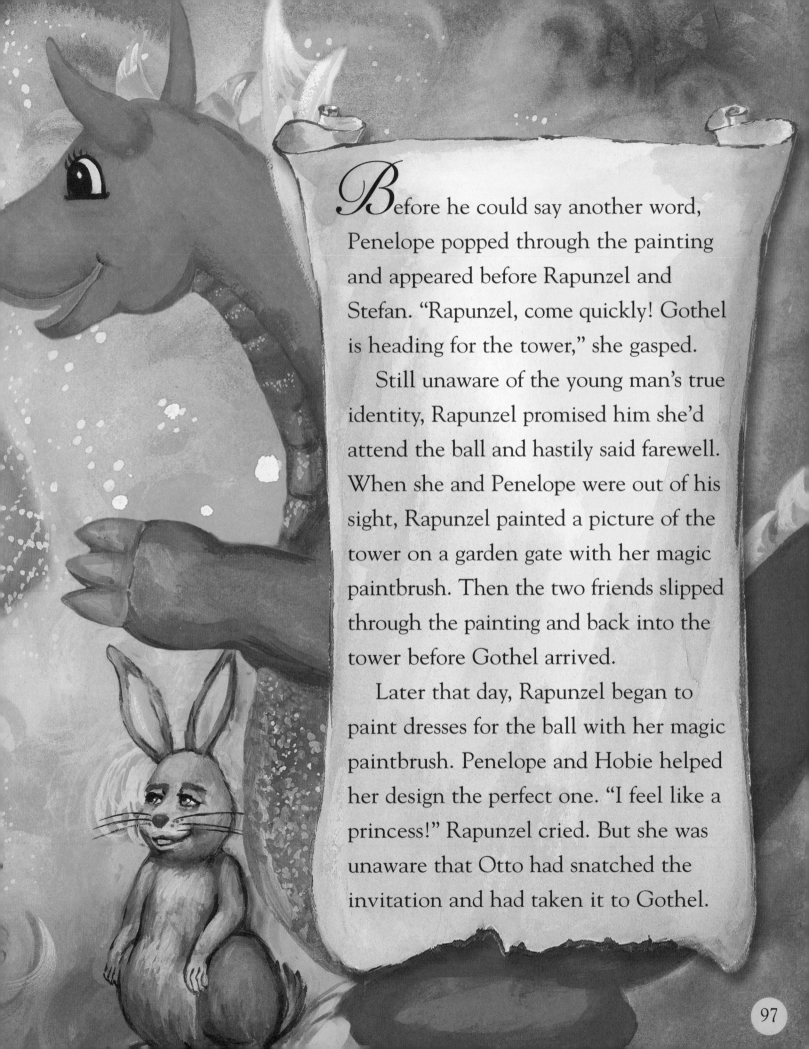

*B*efore he could say another word, Penelope popped through the painting and appeared before Rapunzel and Stefan. "Rapunzel, come quickly! Gothel is heading for the tower," she gasped.

Still unaware of the young man's true identity, Rapunzel promised him she'd attend the ball and hastily said farewell. When she and Penelope were out of his sight, Rapunzel painted a picture of the tower on a garden gate with her magic paintbrush. Then the two friends slipped through the painting and back into the tower before Gothel arrived.

Later that day, Rapunzel began to paint dresses for the ball with her magic paintbrush. Penelope and Hobie helped her design the perfect one. "I feel like a princess!" Rapunzel cried. But she was unaware that Otto had snatched the invitation and had taken it to Gothel.

Gothel was furious when she learned that Rapunzel had escaped again. She stormed into the tower, waving the invitation in the air. "Who gave this to you? Who did you meet?" she demanded.

"Honestly, I-I don't know his name," Rapunzel replied.

"You're lying!" Gothel shouted. Magical bolts flew from her fingertips, cutting off Rapunzel's hair, destroying the painting of the garden, and shattering the magic paintbrush.

Then the witch climbed out the window onto Hugo's back and cast a spell to trap Rapunzel in the tower forever:

Tower, tower, do your part,
Never free your prisoner with a lying heart.
Note that as these words are spoken,
This fearsome spell can never be broken.

An eerie green glint surrounded the tower. Rapunzel was trapped for good without her magic paintbrush.

That evening Gothel went to the masked ball, using Rapunzel's hair to disguise herself. She lured Prince Stefan into the garden, then tore off her mask. "So you're the one meddling in my plans!" she spat.

The prince gasped in horror, "Who are you?"

"I'm the one who's going to teach you to stay away from Rapunzel!" Gothel cackled, throwing magical firebolts at his feet. Prince Stefan dodged the witch's fire, but she chased after him.

Just then, King Wilhelm and his army surrounded King Frederick's castle, surprising all the guests at the ball.

Back at the tower, Penelope had an idea. She and Hobie flew up to the window. "Rapunzel, the spell only traps a prisoner with a lying heart, right? Maybe it won't work on you because your heart is true. You didn't lie to Gothel."

"You could be right," Rapunzel said. And she stepped through the window – right onto the young dragon's back!

Hugo saw that his daughter's friend had a true heart. "Penelope," he said, "take Rapunzel to the ball. I realize now that Gothel is the one who must be stopped."

Penelope took to the air with Rapunzel and Hobie on her back, and they soared across the sky together.

When Rapunzel and her friends arrived at the castle, Rapunzel slipped into the ballroom unnoticed. There, surrounded by guests and soldiers, King Wilhelm and King Frederick were arguing about their long-standing feud.

"You kidnapped my daughter!" King Wilhelm accused King Frederick. "You will pay for –"

"No, I kidnapped her!" Gothel interrupted, making her way through the crowd. She explained she had always loved Wilhelm. But he married another, so in anger she had kidnapped his child and blamed King Frederick to start a feud between the kings and have them destroy each other. "I simply took what was mine," said Gothel.

Rapunzel gasped. She couldn't believe it. King Wilhelm was her father! Gothel caught sight of Rapunzel among the guests and began to chase her.

Rapunzel led Gothel towards the garden, where she had painted a picture of the tower the day before. When Rapunzel reached the open gate, she turned and pleaded, "Please, Gothel, stop all of this. No more hatred! I'll forgive you!"

"Never!" the witch hissed and stormed after her. But as Gothel reached the gate, Penelope and Hobie slammed it shut in front of her, and she was immediately transported through Rapunzel's painting back to the tower. Gothel was trapped forever by her own spell. After all, she was the one with a lying heart.

Rapunzel was reunited with her family. "Your mother and I have never stopped thinking about you," King Wilhelm said. "Our love is as constant . . ."

". . . as the stars above," Rapunzel chimed in.

King Wilhelm and King Frederick made their peace and vowed never to fight again. Rapunzel thought she couldn't be happier, until . . .

She married Prince Stefan. They lived happily ever after in their very own castle – where Hobie had all the carrots he could eat and Penelope and Hugo kept the castle warm all year round.

THE END

Barbie™ of Swan Lake

Barbie stars as Odette, a kind girl who takes pity on a unicorn she sees being chased by villagers. When she follows the unicorn into the Enchanted Forest, the Fairy Queen appears and reveals that Odette's destiny is to save the forest from the evil wizard, Rothbart.

Rothbart turns Odette into a swan, and plots to steal the magic crystal that protects her. With the help of Prince Daniel, Odette finds the courage to stand up to Rothbart and protect the forest.

Barbie™ of Swan Lake

BY
MARY MAN KONG

FROM THE ORIGINAL SCREENPLAY BY
CLIFF RUBY & ELANA LESSER

BASED ON
THE TCHAIKOVSKY BALLET

ILLUSTRATED BY
JOEL SPECTOR

Once upon a time, there was a beautiful girl named Odette. She was sweet and kind, but what she wanted most of all was to be brave.

One day, Odette saw something truly amazing – a unicorn! It was being chased by a group of villagers.

"Wait!" Odette called to the villagers. "You'll hurt it." But the people didn't listen. They wanted to capture the magical creature.

Luckily, the unicorn escaped. Odette followed it deep into the forest. She watched as the unicorn tapped its glowing horn on a rock near a waterfall. Magically, a secret passageway opened, revealing a magnificent lake where fairies and other creatures lived. And they were all talking – including the unicorn!

"Help!" Lila, the unicorn, cried out. The villagers' rope was still tied around her neck.

"Hold still," Odette said. She spotted a crystal in a nearby tree trunk and used its sharp edge to quickly cut Lila's rope.

Suddenly, a beautiful woman appeared. "We've been waiting for you," she said. "I am the Fairy Queen of the Enchanted Forest. And you are the one who has freed the Magic Crystal. You will save our home from the evil Rothbart. He wants to rule the Enchanted Forest and has used his magic to turn people into forest animals."

"You must have me confused with somebody else," Odette said shyly, handing the Magic Crystal to the Fairy Queen. "I'm not brave."

"You're braver than you think," Lila the unicorn said.

"I wish I could help," Odette said, shaking her head. "But I must get back to my family."

Suddenly, an enormous shadow loomed in front of Odette. It was Rothbart! He had seen Odette free the Magic Crystal and knew she would be a threat to him.

Zap! Rothbart aimed his magic ring at Odette and turned her into a swan.

The Fairy Queen quickly placed a crown with the Crystal on Odette's head.

"As long as you wear the Crystal, Rothbart cannot harm you," she said. Rothbart fired his ring at Odette again, but the Crystal glowed brighter and repelled his magic. Realising he could do no more evil, Rothbart left.

"What am I going to do?" Odette asked, looking down at her feathery wings and webbed feet. "Can you turn me back into a human?" she asked the Fairy Queen.

But Rothbart had weakened the Fairy Queen's powers. The Fairy Queen changed Odette back into a human, but only from sunset to dawn. During the day, Odette would remain a swan.

"I have to find a way to break this spell," Odette said.

"The secret is in the Book of Forest Lore," said the Fairy Queen. "It is kept safe by a troll named Erasmus."

Odette and Lila the unicorn quickly followed the Fairy Queen's directions and found the Magic Vault, where the troll lived. Erasmus was happy to help them look for the Book of Forest Lore. They searched and searched, but couldn't find the book anywhere.

Meanwhile, Rothbart was determined to steal Odette's Magic Crystal.

"Odette is a creature of the Enchanted Forest," his daughter, Odile, reminded him. "The Magic Crystal can't protect her from a human."

So Rothbart used his evil powers to lure a human to the forest. He turned himself into a bird and led the hunter, Prince Daniel, all the way to Swan Lake. There the prince saw the swan. He was about to shoot her, but he was spellbound by her beauty. Just then the sun began to set, and the swan was transformed back into Odette. Prince Daniel introduced himself, and Odette told him all that had happened.

Enraged that his plan had backfired, Rothbart raised his ring to blast the prince.

"Stop!" Odette yelled.

"You can save him," Rothbart said. "Give me your crown and I will spare him."

"Never," she said. Odette knew that the Crystal in the crown was more powerful than Rothbart.

"Very well," Rothbart said as he fired his ring at Prince Daniel. Thinking quickly, Odette bravely stepped in front of the prince, and the Magic Crystal protected them both. Rothbart was furious. He left, vowing to get the Crystal somehow.

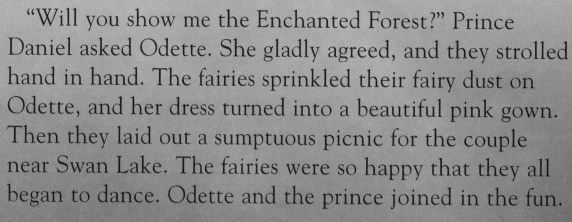

"Will you show me the Enchanted Forest?" Prince Daniel asked Odette. She gladly agreed, and they strolled hand in hand. The fairies sprinkled their fairy dust on Odette, and her dress turned into a beautiful pink gown. Then they laid out a sumptuous picnic for the couple near Swan Lake. The fairies were so happy that they all began to dance. Odette and the prince joined in the fun.

As the prince danced with Odette, he asked her to go with him to his castle. He wanted to protect her, but Odette would not go. She knew she was needed in the forest to help her friends defeat Rothbart. Prince Daniel agreed to leave without her only after Odette promised to attend the royal ball at the castle the next night.

Later that night, Erasmus ran to Odette and the Fairy Queen. He had found the Book of Forest Lore! Inside, they discovered the spell of the Magic Crystal:

The one who frees the Magic Crystal will share
a love so true, so pure, that it will overcome all.
If, however, the true love pledges love to another
the Magic Crystal will lose its power forever.

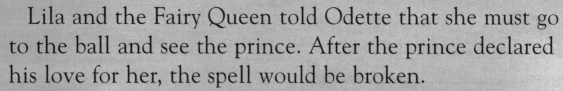

Lila and the Fairy Queen told Odette that she must go to the ball and see the prince. After the prince declared his love for her, the spell would be broken.

The Fairy Queen used her powers to change Odette's clothes into a beautiful swan gown and her crown into a sparkling tiara. And the fairies gave her a glittery necklace. Everyone danced around with joy. They couldn't wait for Odette to go to the ball the next day.

Suddenly, Rothbart swooped down from the sky. He kidnapped Erasmus and took him and the Book of Forest Lore back to his dark palace.

"My, my," Rothbart said as he read the book. "I see the Magic Crystal isn't invincible after all."

Rothbart planned to cast a spell on the prince so that he would think Odile was Odette. If Prince Daniel pledged his love to Odile, the Crystal's power would be lost forever.

The next morning, Odette turned back into a swan. She and her friends went to rescue Erasmus from Rothbart's castle. Odette flew into the palace and brought Erasmus back to the Enchanted Forest. Once the troll was safe, Odette flew to the prince's castle.

At the ball, the prince danced with Odile, thinking she was Odette – thanks to Rothbart's evil spell. Odette flew near the castle to warn the prince about Rothbart's plan. But Rothbart saw her and quickly shut all the windows. She was locked out of the castle!

As the prince danced with Odile, he asked her to marry him – still thinking she was Odette. When Rothbart heard this, he asked Prince Daniel, "Do you love her?"

"Yes, I love her with all my heart," said the prince.

As soon as Prince Daniel uttered those words, the glow of the Magic Crystal slowly started to fade, and the Prince saw who Odile really was. Outside, Odette suddenly changed back into her human form and fell to the ground unconscious. Rothbart dashed over and took the Crystal from Odette's tiara – the Magic Crystal was finally his! He put his prize on a chain and wore it around his neck.

The Fairy Queen and her fairies hurried to bring the injured Odette back to the safety of the Enchanted Forest. Rothbart chased them, but the prince followed, and he and Rothbart engaged in a fierce battle.

"You don't know when to give up, do you?" Rothbart asked as he raised his magic ring.

At that moment Odette woke up and rushed to protect the prince. They tried to shield each other from Rothbart's evil magic. Rothbart just laughed and zapped them with a bolt from his ring. Odette and Prince Daniel fell to the ground, holding hands.

But Odette and the prince's love for each other was so strong and true that the Magic Crystal began to glow brighter than ever. Sparks of lightning shot out of the glowing Crystal and surrounded Rothbart. Soon there was nothing left but the Magic Crystal. Rothbart was gone forever!

"Are you all right?" Odette asked the prince after the spell was broken.

"Yes," said Prince Daniel. "Rothbart tricked me. It's you I love, if you'll have me."

"Oh, yes," Odette said as she threw her arms around the prince.

The Enchanted Forest was saved! Soon there was a huge celebration in honour of Odette and Prince Daniel.

"And you said you weren't brave," said Lila the unicorn.

"A wise unicorn once told me that I was braver than I thought," Odette said with a smile. "And she was right."